This Book Belongs To

_____

This book is dedicated to all those

labeled "disabled"

who believe that the only real disability

in life is a bad attitude.

I'm labeled disabled, but I disagree

I'm tickled to tell you I love being me

I may be unable to do what you do

But step in my world and let me show you...

My life is just slower enabling me

To view all the wonders that most do not see

I think I'd get dizzy so busy I'd be

If I raced around blindly from A to Z

I'm slower in thinking and slower in speech

But none of this keeps me out of reach

Of the goal that I always have in mind

Of showing God's love and being kind

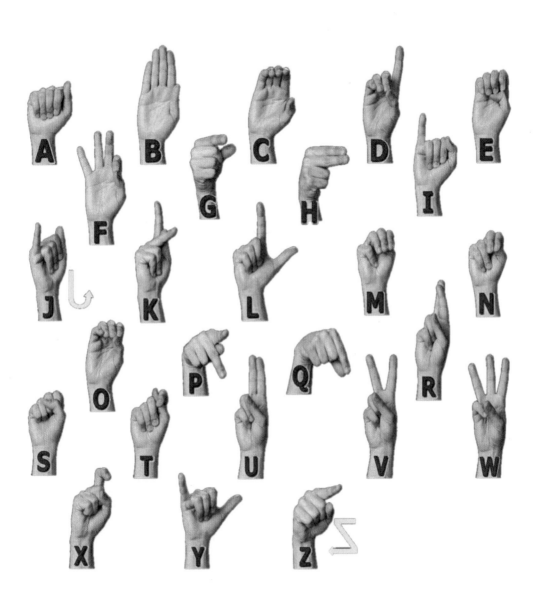

My smiles don't come slowly though—no problem there

My hugs have no limit with plenty to spare

I'm bubbly and cuddly—you really should try it

Most of the time I think life is a riot!

I am unique, unlike the norm

A different mold, a different form

A different language, different moves

But loving ways I'll always choose

I have no reason to lose sleep

Peaceful thoughts are all I keep

My conscience never bothers me

No stress at all—I'm worry free

My angels are encamped about

They're always with me I don't doubt

I feel their presence everywhere

Protecting me with tender care

In church I sing the hymns so true

The words aren't there, but God knows who

Is making such a joyful sound

We're all the same in Him I've found

It's all in how you run your race

Some of us at a slower pace

So as you're racing down life's track

Don't forget us in the back

Just because I'm unlike you

Doesn't mean there's nothing new

That I can teach you now and then

About a different way to win

Sometimes I like what I cannot do

You may wish you couldn't do this too

I've never been able to tell a lie

Or say hurtful things to make someone cry

I've never said something I'd ever regret

That's one thing most people can't say, I bet

I love everybody—I don't hold a grudge

Do I sound disabled? You be the judge

I look at the world through innocent eyes

Magical things are still a surprise

The wonder in life that most take for granted

Will always amaze and keep me enchanted

IQ doesn't measure good heart or great style

There's no bubble for bubbly, no mark for
sweet smile

So "special" I'm called, but you're special too

Disabled or not, that still holds true

So be careful—don't judge by the cover

We're much more than what you can see

Be aware that we're folks just like you are

We all can be friends—you and me!

Made in the USA
Middletown, DE
03 December 2024

66033529R00015